BOOKS WRITTEN AND ILLUSTRATED BY
ROBERT LAWSON

THEY WERE STRONG AND GOOD

BEN AND ME *

I DISCOVER COLUMBUS *

WATCHWORDS OF LIBERTY *

COUNTRY COLIC *

RABBIT HILL

MR. WILMER *

MR. TWIGG'S MISTAKE *

THE FABULOUS FLIGHT *

McWHINNEY'S JAUNT *

MR. REVERE AND I *

CAPTAIN KIDD'S CAT *

BOOKS ILLUSTRATED BY
ROBERT LAWSON

THE STORY OF FERDINAND

WEE GILLIS

PILGRIM'S PROGRESS

THE CROCK OF GOLD

MR. POPPER'S PENGUINS *

POO POO AND THE DRAGONS *

PRINCE PRIGIO *
AND MANY OTHERS

Published by Little, Brown and Company

BEN AND ME

BEN and ME

A New and Astonishing *LIFE* of
BENJAMIN FRANKLIN
As written by his Good Mouse
AMOS ′ ′ ′
Lately Discovered, Edited
& Illustrated by

**ROBERT
LAWSON**

**LITTLE, BROWN
AND COMPANY**
BOSTON

FOREWORD

THE MANUSCRIPT which forms this book was sent me recently by an architect friend. While altering an old Philadelphia house, workmen uncovered a small chamber beneath a bedroom hearthstone. This tiny room, for such it appeared to be, was about eighteen inches square. It contained various small articles of furniture, all of the Colonial Period. In one of these, a secretary desk, was found a manuscript book, the leaves of which, about the size of postage stamps, were covered with minute writing.

With the aid of a powerful reading-glass my friend managed to decipher the story which follows.

Scarce able to believe that such a remarkable document could be other than some ancient hoax, he sent it to various authorities for their opinions.

Scientists of the Brownsonian Institute have assured him that their analyses of the paper and ink prove them definitely to be of Early American manufacture, and that the writing was most certainly done with a quill pen of that period.

More startling still was the report from officials of the National Museum of Natural History, stating that, incredible as it might seem, there could be no possible doubt that the handwriting was that of — a mouse!

So without attempting any explanation, with only a few minor corrections of spelling and grammar, and the addition of some drawings, I give you Amos' story in his own words.

I am aware that his account of Franklin's career differs in many respects from the accounts of later historians. This

I cannot explain but it seems reasonable to believe that statements made by one who lived on terms of such intimacy with this great man should be more trustworthy than those written by later scholars.

Robert Lawson

Rabbit Hill
May, 1939

CONTENTS

BEN AND ME

• 1 •

I, AMOS

SINCE THE RECENT death of my lamented friend and patron Ben Franklin, many so-called historians have attempted to write accounts of his life and his achievements. Most of these are wrong in so many respects that I feel the time has now come for me to take pen in paw and set things right.

3

All of these ill-informed scribblers seem astonished at Ben's great fund of information, at his brilliant decisions, at his seeming knowledge of all that went on about him.

Had they asked me, I could have told them. It was ME.

For many years I was his closest friend and adviser and, if I do say it, was in great part responsible for his success and fame.

Not that I wish to claim too much: I simply hope to see justice done, credit given where credit is due, and that's to me — mostly.

Ben was undoubtedly a splendid fellow, a great man, a patriot and all that; but he *was* undeniably stupid at times, and had it not been for me — well, here's the true story, and you can judge for yourself.

I was the oldest of twenty-six children. My parents, in naming us, went right through the alphabet. I, being first, was **A**mos, the others went along through **B**athsheba, **C**laude, **D**aniel — and so forth down to the babies: **X**enophon, **Y**sobel, and **Z**enas.

We lived in the vestry of Old Christ Church on Second Street, in Philadelphia — behind the paneling. With that number of mouths to feed we were, naturally, not a very prosperous family. In fact we were really quite poor — as poor as church-mice.

But it was not until the Hard Winter of 1745 that things really became desperate. That was a winter long to be remembered for its severity, and night after night my poor father would come in tired and wet with his little sack practically empty.

We were driven to eating prayer-books, and when those gave out we took to the Minister's sermons. That was, for me, the final straw. The prayer-books were tough, but those sermons!

Being the oldest, it seemed fitting that I should go out into the world and make my own way. Perhaps I could in some way help the others. At least, it left one less to be provided for.

So, saying farewell to all of them — my mother and father and all the children from Bathsheba to Zenas — I set forth on the coldest, windiest night of a cold and windy winter.

Little did I dream, at that moment, of all the strange people and experiences I should encounter before ever I returned to that little vestry home! All I thought of were my cold paws, my empty stomach — and those sermons.

I have never known how far I traveled that night, for, what with the cold and hunger, I must have become slightly delirious. The first thing I remember clearly was being in a kitchen and smelling CHEESE! It didn't take long to find it; it was only a bit of rind and fairly dry, but how I ate!

Refreshed by this, my first real meal in many a day, I began to explore the house. It was painfully bare; clean, but bare. Very little furniture; and that all hard and shiny; no soft things, or dusty corners where a chap could curl up and have a good warm nap. It was cold too, almost as cold as outdoors.

Upstairs were two rooms. One was dark, and from it came the sound of snoring; the other had a light, and the sound of sneezing. I chose the sneezy one.

6

In a large chair close to the fireplace sat a short, thick,
round-faced man, trying to write by the light of a candle.
Every few moments he would sneeze, and his square-rimmed
glasses would fly off. Reaching for these he would drop his

7

pen; by the time he found that and got settled to write, the candle would flicker from the draught; when that calmed down, the sneezing would start again, and so it went. He was not accomplishing much in the way of writing.

Of course I recognized him. Everyone in Philadelphia knew the great Doctor Benjamin Franklin, scientist, inventor, printer, editor, author, soldier, statesman and philosopher.

He didn't look great or famous that night, though, he just looked cold — and a bit silly.

He was wrapped in a sort of dressing-gown, with a dirty fur collar; and on his head was perched an odd-looking fur cap.

The cap interested me, for I was still chilled to the bone — and this room was just as bleak as the rest of the house. It was a rather disreputable-looking affair, that cap; but in one side of it I had spied a hole — just about my size.

Up the back of the chair I went, and under cover of the next fit of sneezes, in I slid. What a cozy place *that* was! Plenty of room to move about a bit; just enough air; such soft fur, and such warmth!

8

"Here," said I to myself, "is my home. No more cold streets, or cellars, or vestries. HERE I stay."

At the moment, of course, I never realized how true this was to prove. All I realized was that I was warm, well fed and — oh, so sleepy!

And so to bed.

· 2 ·

WE INVENT THE FRANKLIN STOVE

I SLEPT late the next morning. When I woke my fur-cap home was hanging on the bedpost, and I in it.

Dr. Franklin was again crouched over the fire attempting to write, between fits of sneezing and glasses-hunting. The fire, what there was of it, was smoking, and the room was as cold as ever.

"Not wishing to be critical — " I said. "But, perhaps, a bit of wood on that smoky ember that you seem to consider a fire might — "

"WASTE NOT, WANT NOT," said he, severe, and went on writing.

"Well, just suppose," I said, "just suppose you spend two or three weeks in bed with pewmonia — would that be a waste or — "

"It would be," said he, putting on a log; "whatever your name might be."

"Amos," said I. . . . "And then there'd be doctors' bills — "

"BILLS!" said he, shuddering, and put on two more logs, quick. The fire blazed up then, and the room became a little better, but not much.

"Dr. Franklin," I said, "that fireplace is all wrong."

"You might call me Ben — just plain Ben," said he. . . . "What's wrong with it?"

"Well, for one thing, most of the heat goes up the chimney. And for another, you can't get *around* it. Now, outside our church there used to be a Hot-chestnut Man. Sometimes, when business was rushing, he'd drop a chestnut. Pop was always on the look-out, and almost before it touched the ground he'd have it in his sack — and down to the vestry with it. There he'd put it in the middle of the floor — and we'd all gather round for the warmth.

"Twenty-eight of us it would heat, and the room as well. It was all because it was OUT IN THE OPEN, not stuck in a hole in the wall like that fireplace."

"Amos," he interrupts, excited, "there's an idea there! But we couldn't move the fire out into the middle of the room."

"We could if there were something to put it in, iron or something."

"But the smoke?" he objected.

"PIPE," said I, and curled up for another nap.

I didn't get it, though.

Ben rushed off downstairs, came back with a great armful of junk, dumped it on the floor and was off for more. No one could have slept, not even a dormouse. After a few trips he had a big pile of things there. There were scraps of iron, tin and wire. There were a couple of old warming-pans, an iron oven, three flatirons, six pot-lids, a wire birdcage and an anvil. There were saws, hammers, pincers, files, drills, nails, screws, bolts, bricks, sand, and an old broken sword.

He drew out a sort of plan and went to work. With the clatter he made there was no chance of a nap, so I helped all I could, picking up the nuts and screws and tools that he dropped — and his glasses.

Ben was a fair terror for work, once he was interested. It was almost noon before he stopped for a bit of rest. We looked over what had been done and it didn't look so bad — considering.

It was shaped much like a small fireplace set up on legs, with two iron doors on the front and a smoke pipe running from the back to the fireplace. He had taken the andirons out of the fireplace and boarded that up so we wouldn't lose any heat up the chimney.

Ben walked around looking at it, proud as could be, but worried.

"The floor," he says. "It's the floor that troubles me, Amos. With those short legs and that thin iron bottom, the heat — "

"Down on the docks," said I, "we used to hear the ship-rats telling how the sailors build their cooking fires on board

13

ship. A layer of sand right on the deck, bricks on top of that, and — ”

"Amos," he shouts, "you've got it!" and rushed for the bricks and sand. He put a layer of sand in the bottom of the affair, the bricks on top of that, and then set the andirons in.

It looked pretty promising.

"Eureka!" he exclaims, stepping back to admire it — and tripping over the saw. "Straighten things up a bit, Amos, while I run and get some logs."

"*Don't* try to run," I said. "And by the way, do you come through the pantry on the way up?"

"Why?" he asked.

"In some ways, Ben," I said, "you're fairly bright, but in others you're just plain dull. The joy of creating may be meat and drink to you; but as for me, a bit of cheese — ”

He was gone before I finished, but when he came back with the logs he did have a fine slab of cheese, a loaf of rye bread, and a good big tankard of ale.

We put in some kindling and logs and lit her up. She drew fine, and Ben was so proud and excited that I had to be rather sharp with him before he would settle down to food. Even then he was up every minute, to admire it from a new angle.

Before we'd finished even one sandwich, the room had warmed up like a summer afternoon.

"Amos," says he, "we've done it!"

"Thanks for the WE," I said. "I'll remember it."

· 3 ·

THE BARGAIN

WHEN I WOKE up the room was sizzling warm. Ben was happily writing, as usual, and I went over to see what was going on. So far he had written, with a lot of flourishes: —

An Account of the New Pennsylvania Fireplaces, Recently Invented by Doctor Benjamin Franklin, Wherein Their Construction and Their . . .

"Ben," I said, "we'll have to come to an understanding. Do you recollect your exact words when it worked?"

"Why yes, I do," he admitted, very prompt. He was always fair, Ben was, just overenthusiastic about himself. "As I remember, those words were, 'Amos, we've done it!'"

"Exactly," says I, "'*We've* done it!' 'We' means two: you *and* me. Now let's get things straight, Ben. Fame and honors are nothing to me — cheese is. Also there's my family to consider, twenty-five brothers and sisters in a cold vestry, and hungry. I can be a great help to you, I've proved that. Now what do you propose?"

He looked pretty thoughtful then, and I could feel a quotation coming on. Finally it did. "THE LABORER IS WORTHY OF HIS HIRE," he said.

"I don't labor," I said, "I think. And maxims don't fill empty stomachs. That's not a bad one, itself. Be specific."

Well, we talked it over for some time and Ben was very reasonable about the whole affair — generous too. I think that being comfortably warm, for once, helped that.

We finally made the following Agreement.

Twice a week, rain or shine, he promised to have delivered to the vestry: —

1 two-ounce piece best quality CHEESE.

1 one-inch slice RYE BREAD, fresh.

88 grains unhulled WHEAT.

For myself I was to have as home or domicile to me and my heirs, to have and to hold forever without let or hindrance, with daily subsistence and clothing, in addition thereto: —

1 FUR CAP

On my part, I was faithfully to give and perform to him, Benjamin Franklin, advice, aid, assistance and succor, at all times and under all conditions, and with him constantly to abide, till death did us part, so help me . . .

Ben wrote it all up neat with lots of flourishes, Latin phrases, and seals. Then we both signed it, and shook hands on the bargain.

He was fine about the whole thing, and never used a single maxim. I must say he lived up to it, too. Not once in all the rest of his life did that bread, cheese and wheat fail to reach the vestry twice a week, regular as clockwork.

After that we sat around for a while, basking in the warmth, and I couldn't help thinking how my fortunes had changed in a short twenty-four hours. Here I was in a snug, comfortable home, my family well provided for, with a good friend and an interesting future.

I felt so much at peace with the world that when Ben finally asked, "Amos, what shall we call this affair?" I said, "My friend, the credit is all yours. WE hereby call it the FRANK-LIN Stove."

Then we went to bed.

I was soon comfortably settled in my new home. Ben, who was fairly well skilled with the needle, began to contrive many ingenious little improvements in the fur cap.

There was a small compartment where I could keep a supply of food against an emergency and, of course, a place for sleeping. There was also a peephole at the front through which I could watch where we were going. This was of great value, for the streets of Philadelphia were, at that time, most ill-paved and congested. Ben never had his wits about him and I was often able to prevent him from plunging into a mud puddle or a market cart.

However, the most important improvement that we devised was a small hole in the lining of the cap, just above his left ear. Through this I was able to give him, unnoticed by others, my observations and advice.

Historians have been puzzled at the way Dr. Franklin seemed to know what was going on in the minds of others. He didn't. The things that I discovered and told him made it *seem* as though he did. The only remarkable thing about the whole business was ME.

Ben soon became so dependent on my advice that he seldom ventured abroad without me. The fur cap, which formerly he had used only in inclement weather, he now wore constantly, indoors and out, doffing it only in the privacy of our own room.

This, of course, attracted no little attention, but Ben always enjoyed that.

· 4 ·

SWIMMING

OUR LIFE together went along smoothly, and would have continued to do so had Ben not insisted on indulging in what *I* consider a dangerous, unsanitary and barbarous custom. I refer to swimming.

As the hot summer weather came on we often took long walks in the country which were, to me, most enjoyable. One unusually warm day, when we had come to a secluded spot on the banks of the Schuylkill, Ben suddenly stripped off all his clothing, donned a silly-looking striped garment which he called "bathing trunks," and plunged into the water.

It was only my sudden scream and sharp nip on the ear that prevented him from diving in cap and all.

While he disported in a most ridiculous fashion, snorting and floundering about, I, in the cap, was left perched on his heap of clothing, the prey to any wandering cat, dog, hawk or snake that chanced to come along.

As we walked home that evening, I spoke my mind fully on this ridiculous habit and the dangers to which it exposed me.

"In addition," I said, "your hair is soaking wet, and I shall no doubt contract a frightful cold."

Ben was stubborn about it, though: he was rather proud of his skill as a swimmer and insisted that nothing would happen to me.

Nothing did, for some time, until one afternoon, as I watched Ben diving, snorting and splashing like an overgrown grampus, the thing I dreaded came to pass.

Along the bank came trotting a half-grown mongrel dog, seeking mischief, as is the usual habit of such brutes.

I looked wildly for Ben, but at the moment only the soles of his feet were visible. Fortunately, there were many bushes and small trees thereabout, so I lost no time in scurrying up a small sapling. Here in a broad crotch I settled in comfort to watch the proceedings.

The cur, spying Ben, rushed to the bank, barking furiously. Ben *shoo-ed* and shouted as he floundered frantically toward shore. The pile of clothing next attracted the dog's attention. Nosing it over, he selected the cap—and trotted off with it just as Ben, dripping and panting, slithered up the muddy bank.

With a wild cry of "Amos! Amos!" Ben charged after him.

Apparently, this was just the sort of frolic the dog had been seeking, so for a full quarter-hour he had a jolly romp with Ben. Poor Ben coaxed, pleaded and threatened, but to no avail. Had I not been in such a temper, his ridiculous antics would have been most amusing.

At length, tiring of the game, the mongrel picked up the

cap and trotted off up the riverbank, hotly pursued by Ben — who dashed through thickets and over rocks, with utter disregard of his ill-clad person.

Scarce had they disappeared around a curve in the riverbank when two country yokels appeared on the scene. Noting the pile of clothing and failing to discover its owner they became greatly excited. Their excitement increased on discovering Ben's silver watch engraved with his name.

"The great Dr. Frankling," they shouted, "drownded! Drownded!" — and took to their heels in the direction of Philadelphia, carrying Ben's clothes with them.

It was warm and sunny in my tree, and very quiet now. Far up the river I could still hear occasional sounds of barking. These finally culminated in a terrific outburst of yelps and howls. Then all was silent, and I dozed.

I was wakened by the footfalls of an **approaching** figure which I took to be Ben, but few could have recognized in that ludicrous and bedraggled apparition the famous Dr. Franklin! His legs were muddied, bruised and scratched, his bathing trunks torn, his glasses missing. His wet hair, which hung in long disordered wisps, was surmounted by the fur cap, worn at a drunkenly rakish angle.

As he approached, limping, he kept up a continual sound of finger-snapping, whistling and clucking. "Amos, Amos," he called, "Amos, where are you?" — all the while peering nearsightedly into the bushes along the way. Touched as I was by his fondness for me I could not help a chuckle at his appearance.

I was about to relieve his anxiety when my attention was caught by the approach of a great crowd of people from the direction of Philadelphia. Among them I could discern the Governor, the Mayor and many other prominent citizens, as well as Ben's First Volunteer Fire Brigade.

Ben looked frantically about, but there was no escape save in the water, and of that he had had plenty. So, folding his arms, he attempted to appear as dignified as possible, and awaited their arrival. As he did so, he leaned against the tree in which I had taken refuge. Without a moment's loss I slipped into the cap so gently as to be entirely unnoticed.

As the crowd beheld Ben, everyone broke into shouts of relief and joy, accompanied, however, by not a few snickers. He was surrounded by a milling throng all bent on shaking

his hand and congratulating him. Various articles of clothing were loaned and he was soon decently garbed.

Through it all, however, Ben preserved an appearance of the utmost despondency.

The Governor approached offering his hat, a very elegant affair trimmed with lace and gold braid.

"Permit me, Dr. Franklin," he said, most courteous. "Pray do me the honor to wear this. Your present headgear appears — er — slightly disheveled."

"Never," cried Ben angrily. "This cap shall never again leave my head!" And he reached up both hands to settle it more firmly.

I bit his thumb.

"Amos!" he exclaimed happily.

"Beg pardon?" said the Governor.

"Yes, Amos," I whispered fiercely, "and if you don't get us home quickly you'll hear from me. Your hair is soaking and this cap is so strong of dog I'm half-suffocated!"

Ben brightened up at once, and by the time the procession reached home was as pleased with himself as though he had done something really smart — instead of just scaring half the town to death.

· 5 ·

WE DO SOME PRINTING

ONE OF BEN'S chief interests, of course, was printing. I said that he wrote so much stuff that the only thing to do with it *was* to print it. He felt differently about it though — said it was the foundation of his fortune, THE DISSEMINATION OF KNOWLEDGE was MAN'S HIGHEST CALLING, and so on.

"Consider *Poor Richard's Almanack*," Ben would say.

"Consider the good that has done, for countless thousands. Consider the information — "

"Oh, that thing that tells when the sun rises and sets? What good is THAT to anyone? When the sun's up, it's up. Why read about it in a book?"

"But," said Ben, "consider the maxims it contains — think of the lives that have been molded by their wisdom!"

"Consider them!" I snorted. "Have I ever time to consider aught else? Here we have maxims for breakfast, dinner and supper. Have they molded your life? EARLY TO BED AND EARLY TO RISE, MAKES A MAN HEALTHY, WEALTHY AND WISE. *Bah!* When have you ever been to bed early, or risen early, except when you had insomnia? Yet you're healthy and wealthy."

"Perhaps if I lived by the maxim I should also be — wise," he suggested, meekly.

"That I doubt," said I; "it would require more than a maxim: a miracle, more like. . . .

"Then there's that *horrid* one you wrote: THE CAT IN GLOVES CATCHES NO MICE. There's a fine idea to be putting into the heads of cats, and you my friend!"

"I am sorry about that one — truly," said Ben. "It was

done before your arrival. I shall delete it in the next edition."

"Left to myself," said I, "I'd delete the whole thing."

"That," he said, "would be a great mistake. For many thousands are sold each year at no little profit to us; and profits, Amos, buy bread and leisure — and CHEESE."

There seemed to be some reason in that, so we let the matter drop.

We used to spend a good deal of time at Ben's printing shop, for although he had more or less retired he still loved to putter around among the presses, reading proofs and getting in the way generally. The long afternoons there, while splendid for napping, sometimes were a bit tiresome; so I used to putter about some myself. I stayed well away from the presses, however, having suffered a most painful injury to my tail in one of them.

One afternoon while thus idling about, I came upon the type-forms for *Poor Richard's Almanack,* all set up and ready to print. The first thing to catch my eye was that odious CAT IN GLOVES maxim which Ben, of course, had forgotten to delete.

So I deleted it. It was rather fun picking out the letters and dropping them on the floor, so I continued with a few more alterations.

Each maxim read "As Poor Richard Says" or "Says Poor Richard." Now, there never was any REAL Poor Richard. Ben just made him up, and I always considered it downright dishonest. So wherever the name occurred, I removed it and substituted Amos. This was not vanity on my part, but merely a desire for honesty, for there really *was* an Amos. Besides, it was the only name I could spell.

I spent a happy afternoon, and had time enough left to make a few corrections in the Tide Table, where it appeared wrong to me, as well as some risings and settings of the moon.

I did not bother to tell Ben of these improvements for he was busy with other concerns, but a week later they were brought to his attention in rather dramatic fashion.

In the midst of our after-supper nap came a great rapping at the front door, and the Harbor Master burst in, in a state of utmost terror.

"Fly, Dr. Franklin! Fly for your life!" he shouted.

"Calm yourself, Friend," said Ben. "HASTE MAKES WASTE, you know. What appears to be your trouble?"

"Trouble?" sputtered the man. "Trouble enough, with the harbor filled with ships — aground. Do you realize that this — this THING," waving the *Almanack* under Ben's nose, "predicts high water at ten o'clock; that eighteen ships set sail at ten o'clock; that every last one of them went high and dry aground at ten o'clock? WHY? Because the tide was *low* at ten o'clock! That's why! Do you realize that the Shipmasters are on their way here now — to MOB you? Do you realize that the moon you predicted — "

"Never mind the moon," interrupted Ben, snatching the *Almanack* and quickly running through it. He was frowning and I could hear him mumble, "AMOS says — says AMOS — AMOS says — "

We could hear shouts and the tramping feet of the Shipmasters outside. One or two vegetables mashed against the window. The Harbor Master hid in the closet, but Ben suddenly smiled and, opening the window, calmly stepped out on the balcony.

"Friends," he said, "there has been a great mistake."

35

The crowd agreed with jeers, catcalls and more vegetables.

"But," he went on, "no mistake on Poor Richard's part —
or mine. For this, my friends," — holding up the *Almanack,*
— "this is no *Almanack* of MINE."

"In the TRUE *Poor Richard's Almanack* there are divers
Maxims, Adages, Proverbs, Sayings and Bits of Wit and Information, all spoke by Poor Richard.

"If you will but look with care at this scurrilous counter-
feit of MY *Almanack,* you will find nowhere in it the name

Poor Richard, but only that of one Amos, no doubt a contemptible, ignorant and inaccurate fellow.

"No, my friends, this is but a foul hoax, perpetrated by an envious rival who hopes to thus discredit the true *Poor Richard's Almanack*. Hereafter, always insist on the genuine and accept no substitutes."

There was considerable mumbling and thumbing of Almanacks under the torch light, and one or two voices could be heard to say, "Gum, he's right," and "Good old Ben!"

"Moreover, friends," Ben added, "according to the calculations of the real Poor Richard, whose accuracy has never been questioned, the tide will be high at precisely three thirty-seven o'clock. I should advise, therefore, that you return to your ships with all haste, for they will all soon be afloat."

They hastened off, and Ben saw the still trembling Harbor Master to the door.

When he returned he looked very stern and solemn.

"Amos," he said, "Amos, I smell a rat."

He may have smelled a *rat,* but he certainly saw no *mouse,* for I was well hid under the deepest pile of litter, and there I stayed for two days.

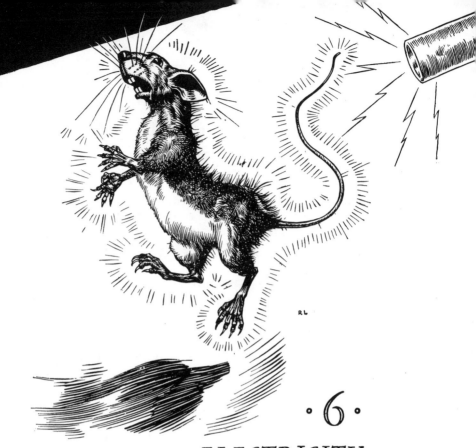

·6·

ELECTRICITY

BEN NEVER thereafter mentioned my little adventure in printing, so I tried to be somewhat more lenient about his maxims.

Trying though they were, however, they were nothing compared to an enthusiasm which beset him about this time. This was the study of what he called "Electricity."

It all started with some glass tubes and a book of instructions sent him by a London friend. These tubes he would
rub with a piece of silk or fur, thereby producing many
strange and, to me, unpleasant effects. When a tube was
sufficiently rubbed, small bits of paper would spring from the
table and cling to it, or crackling sparks leap from it to the
finger of anyone foolish enough to approach.

Ben derived great amusement from rubbing a tube and
touching it to the tip of my tail. Thereupon a terrible shock
would run through my body, every hair and whisker would
stand on end and a convulsive contraction of all my muscles
would throw me several inches in the air.

This was bad enough, but my final rebellion did not come
until he, in his enthusiasm, used the fur cap to rub the tube.
And *I* was in the cap.

"Ben," said I, "this has gone far enough. From now on,
kindly omit me from these experiments. To me they seem a
perfectly senseless waste of time, but if they amuse you, all
right, go ahead with them. Just leave me out."

"I fear that you are not a person of vision, Amos," said he.
"You fail to grasp the world-wide, the epoch-making impor-
tance of these experiments. You do not realize the force — "

"Oh don't I?" I replied. "My tail is still tingling."

"I shall tear the lightning from the skies," he went on, "and harness it to do the bidding of man."

"Personally," said I, "I think the sky's an excellent place for it."

Nothing I could say, though, served to dampen Ben's enthusiasm.

Soon he received an elaborate machine that could produce much greater currents than the glass tubes. It was worked by a crank which he ground at happily for hours. Our room became cumbered with rods, wires, tubes, copper plates and glass jars filled with evil-smelling liquids. It was difficult to move about without touching something likely to produce one of those hair-stiffening shocks.

Ben even went so far as to organize a group of similarly obsessed people, calling it "the Philosophical Society." They gathered once a week, armed with their glass tubes, bits of silk and wires. They spent whole evenings fiddling with these things or listening to long speeches about the wonders of "electricity," mostly by Ben. I napped.

After he had played with the new apparatus for a few weeks and had it working well, Ben decided to give an exhibition of his achievements in this field.

A large hall having been secured for the occasion by the Philosophical Society, Ben spent several busy days arranging and testing his apparatus, planning various experiments, writing a speech and inviting prominent people.

Frankly, I was bored by the whole affair, but since Ben seemed rather hurt by my attitude I tried to take a little interest. I read his speech and the descriptions of all the various experiments. By noon I understood everything quite thoroughly.

While we ate a light lunch of bread and cheese I told Ben of my studies. He was delighted and quite touched by my interest.

In the afternoon he went to have his hair curled, leaving me in the hall, where I went on with my research. Determined that no errors should mar this performance, since it meant so much to Ben, I carefully went over each wire and piece of apparatus, comparing them with his diagrams and descriptions.

I discovered that he had apparently made several grave mistakes, for not a few of the wires were connected in a manner that seemed to me obviously incorrect. There were so many of these errors to rectify that I was kept quite busy all afternoon. My corrected arrangements seemed to leave several loose wires and copper plates with no place to go, so I just left them in one of the chairs on the stage. I was barely able to finish before Ben arrived from the hairdresser's.

As we hurried home for supper, he was so filled with pride

and excitement that I had no opportunity to tell him how narrowly he had escaped ruining the exhibition by his carelessness.

When we arrived back at the hall in the evening the brilliantly lit auditorium was crowded. Seated in chairs on the stage were the Governor and his Lady; the Mayor; several of the clergy; and the Chief of the Volunteer Fire Brigade holding his silver trumpet.

Ben made his speech, and performed several simple experiments with the glass tubes. They were watched with great interest by the audience and generously applauded.

He then stepped to the new apparatus and signaled to a young apprentice from the print shop who was stationed at the crank. The lad turned with a will, and a loud humming sound came from the whirling wheel while blue sparks crackled about it.

"And now, my friends," said Ben proudly, "when I turn this knob you shall see, if my calculations are correct, a manifestation of electrical force never before witnessed on this continent."

They did.

As Ben turned the knob the Governor rose straight in the air in much the same manner that I used to when Ben applied the spark to my tail. His hair stood out just as my fur did. His second leap was higher and his hair even straighter. There was a noticeable odor of burning cloth.

On his third rising the copper plate flew from the chair, landing, unfortunately, in his Lady's lap. Her shriek, while slightly muffled by her wig, was, nevertheless, noteworthy.

The Fire Chief, gallantly advancing to their aid, inadvertently touched one of the wires with his silver trumpet. This at once became enveloped in a most unusual blue flame and gave off a strange clanging sound.

Ben leaped toward them, but I clamped on his ear. I had felt those shocks before.

"The boy — " I hissed. "Stop the machine!"

He sprang at the apprentice, who was still grinding merrily. The lad, not an admirer of the Governor, ceased his efforts with some reluctance.

The Governor was stiff and white in his chair, his Lady moaned faintly under her wig, the Fire Chief stared dazedly at his tarnished trumpet, and the audience was in an uproar.

"Never mind, Ben," I consoled as we walked home, "I feel certain that we'll succeed next time."

"Succeed!" shouted Ben. "SUCCEED! Why, Amos, don't you realize that I have just made the most successful, the most momentous experiment of the century? I have discovered the effects produced by applying strong electric shocks to human beings."

"Granted the Governor *is* one," I said, "we surely did."

THE LIGHTNING ROD

AFTER the Electrical Exhibition most of Ben's acquaintances regarded him rather suspiciously. The Governor even
crossed to the opposite side of the street when we approached.

49

Ben never noticed though, being wrapped-up in more experiments. I observed that he was developing an unseemly interest in lightning.

Every time a house or a tree was struck Ben was the first to reach the scene, questioning all who had been present as to how the bolt had looked, smelled or sounded, what sensations they had felt, and so on. Then he would go into a brown study that lasted for hours, occasionally murmuring, "I wonder, I wonder."

"Wonder what?" I asked finally. It was getting on my nerves.

"Why, if lightning and electricity are the same thing."

"To me they are," I said promptly. "They're both annoying, horrid, dangerous nuisances that should be let strictly alone."

"There you go again, Amos. No vision — no vision."

"All right," I said, "ALL RIGHT. And if they *are* the same and if you *do* prove it, then what?"

"Why then," he said, "why then, I shall go down in history as he who tamed the lightning, who — "

"If you have any notion of making a house-pet of this lightning," I said, "you can go down in history as anything you please. For myself, *I* will go down in the cellar — and stay there."

Two days later I was waked from my afternoon nap by a terrible clatter overhead. Investigation disclosed Ben seated on the roof busily hammering. He had fastened a whole collection of sharp-pointed iron rods to various parts of the housetop. There were two or three on each chimney and a series of them along the ridgepole. These were all connected by a tangle of wires and rods that ran down through the trapdoor into our room.

"You see, Amos," he explained, while connecting wires to various instruments, "the trouble with most people is that they lack the calm observation of the trained scientific mind. Time after time I have rushed to the scene of one of these lightning strokes and all I could gather from the bystanders was that they were 'terrible skeered.'

"Now by collecting a small amount of this so-called 'lightning' with the rods which you saw on the roof and conducting it through wires to these jars and instruments, we shall be able to investigate its nature and behavior with true scientific calm. We shall be able to settle forever the question which is puzzling all great minds, the question of whether or not lightning is electrical."

"It never has puzzled *my* mind," I said. "Left to myself I wouldn't give it a thought."

"Moreover," I continued, "you might as well leave out that 'we.' I resigned from these experiments a long time ago. Any observing that *I* do will be done in the cellar. And as the sky has clouded up rather threateningly I think I will retire there at once."

The storm must have been closer than I thought, for I had barely started for the door when there occurred a most horrifying flash of lightning, followed by a thunder-clap that shook the house to its foundations.

The shock threw me bodily into a large glass jar, luckily empty. This was really fortunate, for here I was able to observe all that went on, while the glass seemed to protect me from the lightning flashes that now followed one another in rapid succession.

At the first flash the liquid in Ben's jars disappeared in a great burst of yellowish steam and the instruments bounced about wildly. As flash followed flash blue sparks ran up and down the wires, the brass andirons glowed as though dipped in phosphorus and streaks of fire shot from the candlesticks on the mantelpiece. The crashing thunder was, of course, continuous, jarring every loose object in the house.

There was now no doubt in *my* mind that lightning was electricity — in its most horrid and dangerous form.

In the confusion I had forgotten Ben. Now, looking about, I was astonished to find him nowhere in sight.

At this moment a large ball of blue fire emerged from the Franklin stove, rolled across the floor and descended the stairs, crackling and giving off a strange odor of sulphur. The unusually violent crash that followed brought a faint moan from the bed.

There I discovered Ben, or rather his feet, for they were the only part of him visible. The rest was covered by the bed-clothes, while two pillows completely muffled his head.

At first I was alarmed, but as each succeeding crash brought an echoing moan and a violent trembling of the feet I realized that all that had befallen him was a severe case of fright.

Safe in my glass jar I thoroughly enjoyed the spectacle of Ben's terror as long as the storm raged.

As the last rumblings died away he cautiously raised

the pillows and peered forth. He was a most amusing sight.

"And now, Dr. Franklin," I jeered as he sheepishly rose from the bed, "would you lend a bit of your calm, scientific study to getting me out of this jar? And by the way, what *did* you observe as to the true nature of lightning?"

"Do you know, Amos," he explained, "that first flash knocked off my glasses, and of course I see very poorly without them."

"So you replaced them with a couple of pillows," I said.

He never answered me — just started picking up the remains of his apparatus.

When, some time later, a scientific writer called them "Lightning Rods," naming Ben as their inventor, he refused to take the credit. This startling display of modesty surprised many people — but not me. I knew all about it.

· 8 ·

THAT KITE

AFTER the disastrous lightning-rod experiment Ben was quite subdued for some days and never even mentioned electricity. I hoped that he was cured of this dangerous hobby, but — alas! my hope was soon to be rudely shattered.

This question of the nature of lightning so preyed upon his mind that he was finally driven to an act of deceit that caused the first and only rift in our long friendship.

I feel sure that brooding on this subject must have seriously affected his mind, for this is the only way in which I can excuse his treacherous conduct.

It came about in this fashion.

One of Ben's favorite forms of relaxation was kite-flying.

On his largest kite he had built for me a tiny platform. Made of light splinters of wood this was securely lashed to the kite just where the sticks of the frame crossed. A stout railing surrounded it and the floor was cushioned with milkweed down, so that a safer or more snug retreat could scarce be imagined.

Sailing aloft in this was a delightful sensation. The gentle motions of the kite, the warmth of the sun and the broad view spread out below all combined to make it a thoroughly restful and enjoyable experience.

A new thrill was added when we contrived a tiny car slung to a pulley running on the kite-string. In this I could cast off from my little porch and go coasting in a long, glorious swoop to Ben and the earth far below.

To this car we later added a small sail, so that when the wind was sufficiently strong I could sail up the string to the

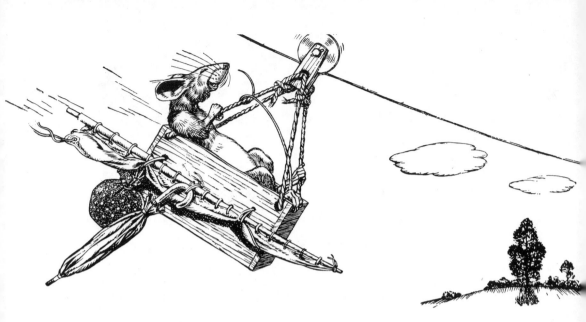

kite. Enabled thus to ascend and descend at will, I spent many happy hours at this thrilling sport.

That Deceit could raise its ugly head in such idyllic surroundings and bring to an end these innocent diversions seems particularly painful. I shall pass over as rapidly as possible the unfortunate happenings which almost brought our friendship to a close.

Ben had hinted that if I were willing to stay aloft during a thunderstorm I could, being so close to the clouds, very easily determine the nature of lightning.

My reply to this proposal was prompt, decided, and in the negative — very strongly in the negative. So much so that Ben dropped the subject and had, I thought, given up the idea completely.

But alas for my trust in human honor! Little did I dream of the horrid plot that this electrical mania was causing to form in his disordered brain!

One hot July afternoon I had ridden aloft and, lulled by the gentle motion and the sun's warmth, had indulged in a long nap. From this I was awakened by a violent tossing of the kite. I at once realized from the black and threatening clouds that a sudden thunderstorm was rapidly approaching, its preliminary gusts already tossing the kite wildly about.

Hastily preparing to descend in my little car, I was horrified to discover that it was not there! Jerks on the string to signal Ben bringing no response, the ugly details of his plot began to dawn on me! I recalled his haste to launch the kite and his incessant talk while doing so, all designed to hide the fact that he had removed the car.

With or without my consent, he had resolved to keep me aloft during the storm!

I sought wildly for some method of descending the string,

but the wind by now was so strong that all my efforts were required to cling to the frail platform.

The next half-hour was the most awful experience of my life. The wild plunging of the kite, the driving sheets of rain, the incessant lightning flashes and the crashing thunder all were so terrifying that I could only hang on and pray.

As shock after stiffening shock ran through my body there was no further doubt in *my* mind as to the nature of lightning. It *was* electrical — decidedly so!

Blue sparks crackled from my whiskers, every hair stood on end and my frame was convulsed by the never-ending shocks.

After what seemed hours of this torture the storm passed and I knew by the motions of the string that the kite was being lowered. Nearing the earth I saw that Ben had taken cover in a shed and was regarding my approach with the greatest eagerness.

Before I had reached the ground he was calling, "Was it, Amos? Was it electricity? WAS it?"

Even had rage not rendered me speechless I should never have given him the satisfaction of an answer. As the kite touched earth I descended and stalked past him in stony silence. Despite his questions and pleadings I pursued my angry way back to town, never pausing until I had reached the shelter of the vestry.

There, after my wondering family had dried me and dressed my burns, I fell into an exhausted sleep that lasted two days.

I woke from this long slumber thoroughly recovered in body, if not in mind, to hear the familiar booming of Ben's voice. I found him seated in the vestry where my mother, flustered by this visit of the family's generous patron, was making a great to-do over him.

My greeting was cold, but Ben was most agreeable and apologetic. He had brought with him our Agreement, which he felt I had broken by leaving him.

"A mere scrap of paper," I snorted, and went on to point out that his electrical craze had not existed when our Agreement was signed, that it alone had caused all our differences and had made life a burden for me. In fact I pointed out things for almost an hour.

"Never," I declared. "Never while this madness lasts will I return to our former association."

Ben finally gave in and agreed to stop all electrical experimenting forever. He wrote it into the Agreement, we signed it and shook hands on the bargain.

With good will restored, my beaming parents brought in a few refreshments and we had a jolly visit. The children were presented to Ben, who was most gracious to them all, patting their heads and asking questions about their schooling and pastimes. Luckily none of them mentioned kite-flying.

"Amos," he said at length, "the reason that I gave up my scientific investigations so readily is this. As you doubtless know, relations between these American Colonies and our Mother Country, England, have become very badly strained. So much so that I have been chosen to go to England and lay our case before the King and Parliament: to attempt to make clear to them the justice of our grievances, to avoid the dangers of rebellion and possibly of war.

"Without you, Amos, I should be lost. Your advice and your wonderful facility for gathering information are more than ever necessary to me. Here is a great opportunity to prove your devotion to your country and to the sacred cause of Liberty. What say you, Amos? I sail at dawn."

It was a solemn moment, but without an instant's hesitation I sprang to my feet.

"Liberty forever!" I shouted. "I'm with you, Ben. Besides, I understand that the English cheeses are of excellent quality."

In the cold, gray damp of the early morning I was at the dock where our ship lay in readiness to sail. Suddenly I noted a long line of ship-rats filing ashore, laden with their belongings.

"Here is an unlucky sign," I thought and hastened to ask the reason for their desertion.

One of the rats, an old gray-bearded fellow, pointed glumly to the tops of the masts. "Them," he said.

Peering aloft I made out, fastened to the top of each mast, one of those hated iron rods.

"Lightning-rods," I muttered.

"That's what HE calls 'em," growled the old graybeard. "Down here all day yesterday he was, putting them up. Conwinced the Capting they'd protect the ship from lightning.

64

I don't hold with no such newfangled notions, I don't. I'm through."

At that moment Ben came puffing down the dock laden with bags, late, as usual.

"Ben," I demanded, pointing to the mast tops, "WHAT are those?"

"Why those — Amos — why those are just — Oh never mind — just hurry aboard like a good fellow — I'll explain those later."

"Explain them to the sharks," I said, turning on my heel.

"But Amos," he protested, as the sailors hurried him up the gangplank, "our agreement!"

"Our agreement," I shouted back, "says *No experiments!* Good-by, Ben, and good luck. 'LIBERTY FOREVER' — but no lightning-rods!"

So I returned to the vestry and Ben sailed alone.

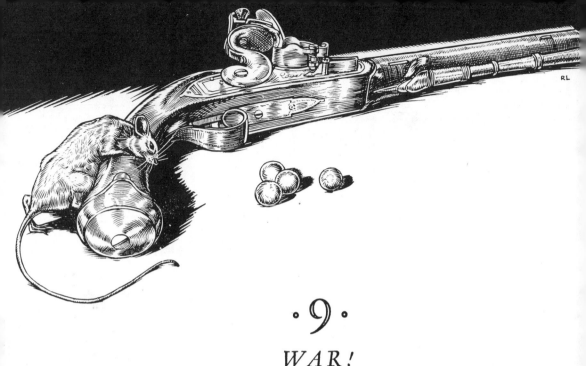

·9·

WAR!

LIFE AT the vestry seemed very quiet after the excitement of living with Ben, but I felt the need of a little quiet just then and the long days with my family were most enjoyable.

Though life at the vestry was quiet, Philadelphia as a whole was not. Restless crowds filled the streets and there were rumors of violence. There was loud talk of stamp taxes and other outrages of the English Government. I gathered that Ben's mission to England was a complete failure.

The War finally started at some place in the province of

Massachusetts, and I thirsted to do what a mouse could to aid the struggling Colonies. There seemed little I could do, however, without Ben; and it gave me great pleasure to hear that he was about to arrive home.

All our differences were forgotten in the face of the dangers that threatened our country and we plunged into our work with the greatest energy.

As far as I was concerned the War of the Revolution was nothing but committee meetings. Ben was on dozens of committees. They met at all hours of the day and night and I was kept so busy rushing about gathering information that I often longed for the old days of lightning-rods and other electrical catastrophes.

Our most important committee was one formed to write what they called a "Declaration of Independence." There were five on the committee, besides me, but the only ones who counted were Ben and Mr. Thomas Jefferson of Virginia. Mr. Jefferson was a talker for fair, almost as bad as Ben, and they would never have made any progress had it not been for me and Red.

Red had come up from Virginia with Mr. Jefferson — in

his saddlebag. Like his patron he was redheaded, a fiery revolutionist, and a great talker.

Scarce had they arrived before Red began preaching Revolution to the mice around the Inn stables. He soon had them organized and led them on several forays which caused the innkeeper considerable trouble with his guests.

In spite of his radical tendencies I could not help liking this young firebrand. We became fast friends, and I introduced him to many prominent Philadelphia mice of my acquaintance, who, though somewhat shocked at the violence of his theories, all admired his eloquence and capacity for leadership. This group held many interesting meetings in Red's saddlebag home, at which the problems of the day were discussed.

At one of these meetings Red brought forth for discussion a "Manifesto," or list of grievances which he felt we mice had suffered at the hands of our master, Man.

It began: "*When in the course of human events it becomes necessary for a mouse to dissolve the bands which have linked him to his master . . .*" and went on at considerable length.

While some of those present felt that our wrongs were slightly overdrawn, everyone was impressed by the force of

Red's writing. So deeply was I moved that I borrowed it to read to Ben.

This I did after his committee had adjourned at a late hour, having accomplished nothing. As I proceeded with the reading Ben showed increasing signs of excitement. At its close he burst out with pleasure:

"Splendid, Amos, splendid!" he exclaimed. "It fits our case exactly. *'When in the course of human events . . .'* Magnificent! Just copy it down, like a good fellow — of course changing the word 'mouse' to 'man' wherever it occurs."

"Are we mice or are we men?" I said. "Copy it yourself, I'm sleepy."

He did copy it and the next day it was adopted by the other members of the committee, all very much pleased with themselves for producing such a splendid document.

Red, of course, was in a fury and orated for hours about this theft of his labors, but we all thought it a rather good joke on him.

When, on the Fourth of July, it was adopted by the Congress as the "Declaration of Independence," there was a great celebration in Philadelphia. Bells rang, bands played and men and boys paraded the streets shooting guns, pistols and fire-crackers — a most terrifying racket.

Ben, of course, joined in these sports despite my protests, and was noisier than any of the youths. He managed to burn most of his fingers, but when he singed my tail severely with a firecracker I finally rebelled, threatening to reveal who had really written this Declaration.

He quieted down then.

· 10 ·

LA BELLE FRANCE

OF COURSE during these stirring times I came in contact with all the great men of the Colonies. The one who impressed me most was, naturally, General George Washington.

Not only was he a magnificent figure of a man and soldier, but the wheat grown at Mount Vernon was of a superb quality. There were always a few grains to be found in his boot-tops and pocket flaps. Quite a few crumbs too, so I always looked forward to seeing him.

On one of his visits to Ben, however, he appeared greatly cast down.

"The situation of our Colonies, Dr. Franklin," he said, "is becoming desperate. Our brave soldiers lack shoes and uniforms, powder and arms. I fear that we must appeal to some foreign power for aid. But to what country shall we appeal? That seems to be the question. Of course there is Spain."

"*French pastry,*" I whispered in Ben's ear.

"And of course France," said Ben.

"There is Russia," suggested the General.

"*French wines,*" I hissed.

"And France," said Ben.

"There are Denmark and Sweden," the General said.

"*Beautiful ladies,*" I whispered.

"France," said Ben. "*Undoubtedly* France!"

"Very well," said General Washington, "France it seems to be. Dr. Franklin, will you go to the Court of France to plead our cause? It is a heavy responsibility for on your success depends our whole hope of victory."

Ben rose. "We will, General, we will," he said determinedly.

"*We?*" asked the General.

72

"I mean I — of course — *I* will," replied Ben. "When do we — I mean I — sail?"

"At once," said the General, rising and looking very noble. "The armed sloop *Reprisal* is ready to sail. With you, Dr. Franklin, will go the hopes and prayers of a new Nation, the ideals, the aspirations — "

"AND Amos," I added, but he didn't hear me.

So we sailed and the less said about the trip the better. I always did despise water and the Atlantic Ocean contained more ugly, gray, unpleasantly churned-up water than I ever dreamed could exist. I was seasick — awfully seasick; and just to make things worse, Ben was not. He was disgustingly well and annoyingly active.

He had a new theory for setting the sails which he told the Captain would greatly increase our speed. This kept him on deck for several days, to my great relief, but was suddenly ended by a tremendous outburst of profanity on deck. Ben entered our cabin, hastily, followed by angry rumblings from the Captain.

"No vision, Amos," he said sadly. "No vision."

"Blurg!" I said.

· 11 ·

AT COURT

OUR VOYAGE at last ended, although I was too far gone
to know or care. By the time I had recovered we were comfortably lodged in a house at Passy, a small town on the out-
skirts of Paris.

Ben, for some unaccountable reason, proved to be tremendously popular with the French people. Scholars, scientists and writers flocked to the house. They hung on his every word and talked of his lightning-rods and kite-flying as though they were something wonderful. Pictures of him were sold in all the shops, while his maxims were quoted everywhere — in French, of course. To me they made even less sense in French than in English.

As for the admiration of the French ladies, it was just plain silly. They swarmed around him like flies around a honeyjar. They all called him "Papa" and used to cry if he refused their invitations to tea or dinner. Our mail was filled with their ridiculous notes, all highly perfumed.

Some of the ladies went so far as to copy the untidy way in which he wore his hair, while others wore fur caps made in imitation of Ben's. One of them even tried to borrow my home for her milliner to copy. I put a stop to that promptly.

We were surrounded by diplomats, politicians and spies, all of whom were trying to find out what Ben was doing in France and, if possible, to prevent him from accomplishing it. Naturally, I was kept extremely busy watching all these people, and telling Ben what they were up to.

I became familiar with the desk of every Ambassador in

Paris, read each one's mail and listened to all their conversations.

Of course, with the information I supplied, Ben was able to thwart every plot against us, thereby gaining the reputation of being a brilliant diplomat.

While I worked myself to a shadow, he was growing fat on all this attention — not to mention the dinners he continually attended.

He *did* do his part at Court, however. The King and Queen were just as silly as the rest of the French in their admiration for Ben, his maxims and his "quaint" clothing. They especially liked the fur cap which, of course, he wore everywhere. By flattery and smooth-tongued promises he managed to borrow millions of francs for General Washington and his ragged army. As long as he secured these vast sums for the cause of Liberty and Justice I didn't mind how ridiculous he made himself, but the sociability was wearing me down.

"Ben," I said, finally, "I've just been thinking of one of your maxims: HE THAT GOES A–BORROWING GOES A–SORROWING. Now here you've come on one of the biggest borrowing expeditions of the age, but where's the Sorrowing? You've borrowed millions from the King of

France and you're still the most carefree old rapscallion I've ever seen. Every evening it's dinner with Madame this or the Countess that."

"FOOLS MAKE FEASTS AND WISE MEN EAT THEM," says he.

"All right," I said, "ALL RIGHT, I won't try to match maxims with you, but this dinner thing is wearing me out, especially that Madame Helvetius. She and her cats!"

"She has many important people at her dinners," he protested.

"She also has CATS," I said, "dozens of cats, all over the house; and that pesky little yapping dog! My nerves are on edge all the time I'm there, Ben; I just can't stand much more of it. Besides, suppose something horrid were to happen to me? How could *you* get along? What would happen to our mission — to our army — to General Washington?"

Ben looked thoughtful. "There is much in what you say, Amos, FOREWARNED IS FOREARMED. Moreover I dislike those cats as much as you do, and as for that dog — Yes, you are right, Amos; it is too grave a risk. From now on we must dine less often with Madame Helvetius and more often perhaps with Madame Brillon."

"Now," I said, "you show some glimmer of sense. If we *must* dine out all the time, let it be Madame Brillon, by all means. There's a lady for you: not a cat in the entire house — good food too."

So to my great relief we ceased our visits to Madame Helvetius and her cats, dining several times a week with Madame Brillon. This suited me perfectly, for in addition to the good food and charming surroundings there was Sophia.

Sophia was a very beautiful white mouse from the Court of Versailles. An aristocrat and a lady, if I ever saw one. . . . A lady in distress, as I soon learned. . . . She lived in Madame Brillon's towering headdress, which made a really dainty home, very different from my rough frontier-cabin type of residence.

During the long tiresome dinners we visited back and forth a great deal. Her English was excellent, for she was beautifully educated, so we were able to converse freely. Having spent most of my life in the company of rather lowly church and tavern mice, I found her brilliant mind and delightful manners a revelation. I soon became her devoted admirer and slave.

Well had she need of an agile mind and a strong right arm, for she had been a victim of the most villainous intrigues and persecution by the white mice of the Court.

The story of her wrongs, which she unfolded to me, is too long to be set forth here. It is enough to say that as a result of a foul conspiracy her husband, a member of one of the oldest mouse families of France, had been exiled to America, while she herself had been obliged to flee from the Court, leaving their seven children captives at Versailles. Her poor husband was now in Philadelphia struggling valiantly to make a home in the New World for his family, should they ever be reunited.

Sophia when banished from the Court had sought refuge with Madame Brillon, whose kindness to the unfortunate was well known. Here, in her protector's great white wig, Sophia served her in much the same capacity that I did Ben. As adviser and confidante she was of the greatest value to her patroness and since Madame Brillon often attended the Court, Sophia was able occasionally to secure news of her children's welfare. Although never able to see them, she learned that they were held in a small cell directly beneath the Queen's

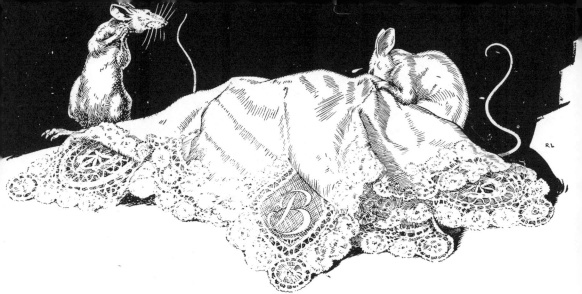

throne. Her one desire in life now was to rescue these unfortunate young ones and join her husband in America, but the task seemed well-nigh hopeless.

Not only was I touched by her beauty and helplessness, but all my Republican sympathies cried out against these wicked injustices by the pampered aristocrats of a dissolute Court.

"Madame," I cried, "do not despair! Though of humble birth I have played no small part in the affairs of men and Nations. What a mouse can do, I will! I, Amos, solemnly swear never to rest until your wrongs are righted and you are happily joined with your children and husband in our beautiful city of Philadelphia, U.S.A."

Tears filled the beautiful pink eyes at my words.

"Oh, Monsieur Amos," she said softly, "could you but accomplish this, what happiness would you bring to a bereft family."

"Fear not, Madame," I said. "To a true son of Liberty and Justice, such a task is a mere nothing. Have courage — and trust in Amos!"

· 12 ·

PLANS

ALTHOUGH I had spoken so boldly to Sophia, the task that I had set myself seemed, on reflection, well-nigh an impossible one. For one mouse to defy the entire Court of France — rescue seven captive children from beneath the very throne of the Queen, and then transport them and their mother to America — appeared to be more than even *I* could accomplish.

But events played into my hands.

Suddenly we received the glad news of Lord Cornwallis' surrender! General Washington and our gallant army were victorious! The War was ended! The Colonies were free!

We celebrated that night, Ben and Me, over cheese and ale, so thoroughly that, to tell the truth, I was rather indisposed the next day and Ben had an attack of gout that lasted a week.

Of course I was all eagerness to leave for home at once. Our long residence among the French, whose foreign ways I always did detest, and the separation from my family, had proved very trying. I also thirsted to fulfill my pledge to Sophia, now that my duty to General Washington was done; but Ben showed no inclination to depart.

He was having such a good time being admired, dining out and showing off at Court that I could not get him even to consider our return to America. Every time I brought up the subject he put me off with one excuse or another, usually accompanied by a maxim. He was really very irritating.

85

But when the King and Queen of France announced that a great ball would be given in his honor on the Fourth of July, he became positively unbearable. He fluttered about from one tailor to another as excitedly as a young belle preparing her trousseau. The house became infested with hairdressers and shirtmakers. He even had his nails manicured. This was really alarming.

Worry and irritation over his behavior must have sharpened my wits, for I soon conceived a Plan that promised to solve all our problems. Completely washing my hands of Ben and his ridiculous antics I plunged into my preparations with intense energy.

Calling together all the peasant mice of Passy, where we lived, I told them the story of Sophia's wrongs and revealed the details of my Plan. With one voice they promised their support. They were a rather stupid, timid lot, but being downtrodden and half-starved they naturally hated the aristocrats of Versailles.

Next I visited several of the Embassies, where, in the course of my spying activities, I had made many acquaintances.

The Russian mice were wild, uncouth fellows, but terrible fighters and always ready for an affray. They answered my plea for aid with enthusiastic shouts. The Swedes were next. Stalwart, steady, powerful warriors, I counted on them greatly and was overjoyed when, after soberly considering my speech, they promised their assistance.

I also managed to enlist the services of a few Italian and Spanish mice, but knowing their erratic temperaments, did not count on them greatly. I placed my main reliance on the Swedes and Russians.

How I longed for Red Jefferson! How invaluable his flaming speeches, his inspiring leadership would be at such a moment!

My joy knew no bounds when Ben announced at dinner that Mr. Thomas Jefferson was arriving in Paris that night.

Surely Red would be with him?

"Mr. Jefferson is to be America's first Ambassador to France," said Ben rather sadly; "and I, I suppose, will no longer be necessary here."

"I've been telling you that for several months," I replied. "Perhaps Mr. Jefferson can convince you of it. . . .

"Never mind, Ben," I went on, for he looked pretty hurt. "Think of the Fourth of July Ball. You'll be the center of attention there, certainly."

He cheered up then and resumed his foppish preparations, leaving me free to continue my own arrangements.

Surely enough Red arrived that night with Mr. Jefferson. Fiery and rebellious as ever, he fell in with my plans at once. He fairly boiled with rage when I recounted the tale of Sophia's wrongs at the hands of the Palace crew.

"Patricians!" he snorted. "Aristocrats! Oppressors! Despots! Vultures! . . . Liberty and Justice, Amos! Tell me your plans. When do we strike?"

Together we went over every detail of my preparations. Red approved of all that I had done and had several excellent suggestions of his own.

"Our forces, Amos," he said, "are weak for such an undertaking. The White Mice of Versailles are known to number many hundreds, perhaps thousands. Pampered fops though they are, there are many skilled swordsmen among them. Your Russians and Swedes are good, but few in number. The peasant mice of Passy are uncertain, prone to panic. What would I not give for a handful of good, true-blue Yankees!"

A really brilliant thought struck me.

"John Paul Jones!" I shouted. "His fleet is at the port of Lorient. His ship-rats are the greatest fighters in the world. One of his Lieutenants is in Paris now and returns to Lorient tonight. I shall send a plea for assistance in his cocked hat! They will not fail us!"

"Splendid, Amos!" exclaimed Red. "Splendid! I, also, have had a thought. The downtrodden Slum Mice and Sewer Rats of Paris are ripe for Revolution! Starved and oppressed, they have long chafed under the tyranny of these mincing Patricians. All that they lack is a leader. *I* will be that leader. LIBERTY FOREVER!"

89

His red fur bristling with energy, he dashed off into the night, while I busied myself with the message to the ship-rats of John Paul Jones.

Ben came in before I had finished and began to preen himself before the mirror.

"A delightful evening, Amos, delightful. You really should have been along. Charming people — witty conversation — "

"By Dr. Franklin, I suppose," said I.

"My new waistcoat was greatly admired," he went on.

"Don't bother me," I snapped testily, "I have no time for mincing popinjays, *I'm* busy."

"*Busy?*" he asks. "Why Amos! This is the time of Peace. The time to cultivate the finer things of life. The War is over."

"That's what *you* think!" I said. "Good night — and horrid nightmares."

· 13 ·

THE BATTLE
OF VERSAILLES

JULY FOURTH arrived and found my preparations complete. Red Jefferson came to report late in the morning. His disheveled fur and red-rimmed eyes indicated sleepless nights of effort, but he was, as always, brimful of energy and enthusiasm.

"All is in readiness, Amos," he said. "The sewers are in a turmoil! Revolution and Liberty fill the air! Vengeance is on every tongue! I can scarce restrain their ardor!"

"See that you do," I said. "One false move would ruin everything. Remember now — the third south window of the Throne Room. Here is your map of the Palace grounds. The night will be warm and all windows open. The signal is UP AND AT 'EM! — and not a move or a sound before that signal. I am depending on you."

Red glanced grimly at the cudgel with which he had armed himself.

"I had a winter at Valley Forge under Von Steuben," he said. "I know something of discipline. Trust me, Amos. LIBERTY AND JUSTICE FOREVER!"

He was off again and I thanked the Providence that had sent me this dynamic lieutenant.

In the afternoon I visited Sophia for last-minute instructions. Although trembling slightly with excitement, she retained the poise of the true aristocrat.

"The Russians and Swedes will report to you," I told her, "they are the most dependable. I myself shall take charge of the Passy peasants, who require a firm hand. How about the headdress?"

"A splendid one for our purpose, Monsieur Amos," she said. "Would you care to see it?"

Peering through a curtain we could see three hairdressers and two maids arranging Madame Brillon's headdress for the ball.

I had seen many elaborate hair arrangements at the Court, but this far exceeded anything I had ever beheld. The powdered curls, rising to a height of four feet above her head, were arranged to represent the waves of the Ocean. Surmounting these was a full-rigged ship with an American flag at the masthead. Long red, white and blue ribbons, inscribed LIBERTY AND JUSTICE, flew from the bowsprit. Just below the ship was a colored wax medallion of Ben, upheld by pink Cupids and decorated with some silly sentiment.

"Perfect!" I said. "The ship will hold all the Swedes. They are great sailors and will feel at home there. The Russians you will have to take inside, unfortunately. They are a bit uncouth."

"This is not a moment to worry about daintiness," she replied calmly.

"You are splendid, Madame," I exclaimed. "Courage now, and trust in Amos. Remember the signal — UP AND AT 'EM. Not a sound or a movement before that! Fear not, all will be well!"

"Bless you, Monsieur," she said bravely; "LIBERTY AND JUSTICE."

The peasant mice reported to me early in the evening. They were rather a motley crew, armed with scythes, clubs and other crude weapons. I had drilled them as well as possible, but had no great confidence in their steadiness. I did try to impress on them the need for absolute obedience and silence.

Ben, of course, was in a twitter of excitement over his new clothes. This was fortunate, for I was able to stow all my awkward band aboard him without attracting his attention. As a matter of fact, in his state of excitement, a swarm of bees could have traveled in his cap and he never would have noticed.

Twelve of us occupied the fur cap, I being stationed at the peephole in front. The rest I secreted in various pockets. One clever little fellow clung to Ben's watch-fob, where he gave the appearance of being a charm or ornament of some sort.

Once we were safely started for the Ball, I gave a sigh of relief. All seemed to be going well. True, there was no word from the ship-rats of John Paul Jones, but I had done all I could. We must do our best without them.

The Palace of Versailles was a scene of the greatest gaiety. Lights were everywhere, fireworks filled the sky, orchestras played. The great halls were crowded with guests, all come to honor the United States — and Ben.

The lights, the opulent costumes, the sounds and splendors of the Court, brought a great chattering from my country-bred cohort, which I sternly suppressed.

We paused briefly at the entrance to the Throne Room while a path was cleared for Ben and I had a moment to glance around. Among the throng I spied Madame Brillon. From the slight quivering of her towering headdress I knew that Sophia's contingent was present. A glimpse of Red's flaming head on the third south window sill reassured me that he and his mob were faithful.

Ben, of course, was the center of all attention. Every eye was upon him as we advanced slowly up the length of the great hall.

As we approached the magnificent throne where the King and Queen sat, I nudged the leader of my peasants. "Ready," I muttered. I could feel Ben trembling with excitement as he halted to make his bow.

At that tense moment I leaned from the peephole and shouted in my loudest tones the agreed signal: "UP AND AT 'EM!"

Ben fairly dripped mice!

My peasant regiment swarmed from his coat, his hat, his waistcoat. Forming in company-front at his feet, as I had trained them, they charged toward the Queen's throne.

A scene of the wildest confusion followed. The Queen and twenty-seven of her courtiers promptly fainted. The King, pale and trembling, rose from his throne and rushed toward the window, only to be met by Red and his shrieking rabble of slum mice and sewer rats. Thereupon the King also fainted and was rather badly trampled by the fleeing ladies of the Court.

The white mice of the Palace Guard, although taken by surprise, soon rallied, driving back the first charge of my undisciplined peasants. But now the Swedes and Russians joined the fray and the battle raged fiercely about the ankles of the Queen. Alas for Red's faith in the proletariat! At the first sight of the lavish refreshments spread out in the adjoining rooms his fickle Revolutionists dropped their weapons and rushed for the food.

Screaming with rage and disappointment Red dashed into the fray. His flashing cudgel and flaming fur were always in the thickest of the fighting.

One by one the peasants of Passy deserted and joined in demolishing the refreshments. The Swedes and Russians, led by the intrepid Red, battled doggedly, but the tide was turning against them. From every corridor of the Palace came swarms of white mice to reinforce the ranks of the enemy. Inch by inch we were being forced back from our goal, the cell where Sophia's children lay.

Amid the confusion of the conflict I was suddenly aware of a clear, thin, piping sound.

Could it be? Yes, surely it was! Through the hot summer

air came the shrill scream of a fife. And the tune was YANKEE DOODLE!!

Through the window they came piling — the sailor rats of John Paul Jones! Fifty fighting Yankees! LAFAYETTE, WE ARE HERE!

Flashing cutlasses and flailing handspikes drove through the throng. The white mice fled like snowflakes before a wind. In no time the cage was captured, the door demolished and Sophia's children brought forth, free mice!

A grizzled old bosun pulled his forelock.

"Cap'n Jones's compliments," he said. "Any further orders?"

Red appeared, dripping sweat and blood, eyes flashing.

"Orders?" he shouted, "orders? Yes, by Heaven!" He pointed to the refreshment room. "That rabble! That scum! Clear them out!"

"Aye, aye sir," said the bosun. The cutlasses flashed and the deserters fled, shrieking, before them.

"It's yours, boys!" said Red. "Help yourselves."

And then to me, "I'm done, Amos," and slumped to the floor.

Madame Brillon had fainted, out of politeness to the Queen. We rescued Sophia from the wreckage of the headdress and it did my heart good to see her joyous reunion with the seven children.

Poor Ben! Looking perfectly dazed, he stood alone in the center of a large empty space. Everyone had crowded away from him as though he were infected with the plague. The King, by now recovered, was conferring with a group of his Generals, all of whom were darting angry glances at Ben. I began to fear for his safety.

With Sophia's assistance I managed to get the half-conscious Red into the fur cap; then Sophia and her happy brood climbed aboard.

"Ben," I suggested, "don't you think we had best be getting home? You seem to have lost a great deal of your popularity."

We left, by a rear door, still shunned by all present. As we passed the refreshment room Sophia and the children waved happily to their rescuers, who were boisterously celebrating the victory. The grizzled bosun led them in three hearty cheers, and we left the Palace with the roaring chorus of A YANKEE SHIP AND A YANKEE SKIPPER ring·ing in our ears.

"The French, Ben," I said, "are a fickle people. One moment you're a hero and the next an outcast. When do we sail for home?"

He seemed still in a daze.

"I don't know, Amos," he said uncertainly. "Whenever you say, I guess."

· 14 ·

HOME

THE VOYAGE home was made most pleasant for me by the gracious presence of Sophia and her charming children.

Ben, however, was quite downcast. He had gone to the Palace of Versailles the day after the great battle and had been severely snubbed. The guard, indeed, had been quite rude, making some unpleasant remark about "people who shed mice." All his Ladies and Countesses had also refused to admit him.

"But, Ben," I said, "don't you realize that our own country of America is waiting to welcome you back as a hero?"

"Do you really think so, Amos?" he asked, brightening up. "Will I — will we — be heroes?"

"Of course we will," I said. "Haven't we raised the money for the whole War of Independence? Why, General Washington himself will probably be at the dock to meet us. There'll be bands, and parades — "

"Maybe you're right, Amos," he said, all cheered up again. "Do you think there'll be fireworks?"

Our reception was everything that even Ben could have hoped for. There were salutes of cannon and firearms, there were delegations from Congress and a message from General Washington. The Mayor, the City Council and the First Volunteer Fire Brigade were all present, dressed in their best uniforms. There were floats, addresses, bands and a parade.

Ben, of course, occupied the first carriage, beaming with pride. As usual, he wore the old fur cap, now so ancient and threadbare that there were plenty of peepholes for Sophia and me and all the seven children. They, naturally, were in a state of the greatest excitement, what with the bands, the crowds, and their first sight of the New World. Sophia retained her usual well-bred dignity, but her pink eyes sparkled with joy at the prospect of rejoining her husband.

He was awaiting our arrival at Ben's house, and my first glance assured me that he was a worthy husband and father for this charming family.

I left them to their new-found happiness and accompanied Ben to a great Banquet that was being given in his honor by the City Council.

During the long, wordy speeches I lay in the cap and thought over the events of the last few years. I had done my duty to General Washington, I had contributed no little to our victory in the War so recently won: the Colonies were free. I had redeemed my promise to Sophia, rescued her children and reunited her family. Ben was now old enough to keep out of trouble — fairly well. "At last," I thought, "I can relax. Before us lies a peaceful and uneventful old age.

"I must be getting old," I thought sleepily, as Ben's voice boomed and meandered on, describing his brilliant triumphs in France; "I can even stand these dinners."

Then I slept.

I was perfectly right about getting old. We *were* old. I found more and more pleasure in staying quietly at home where I could enjoy the company of Sophia's children. Their father had prospered in the New World. He had established a most comfortable home for his family in a house not far from Ben's, and a delightful household it was.

Many of the Court customs that they had brought from France, especially their fondness for dancing all night, were considered somewhat frivolous by the more staid Philadelphia mice, but their gaiety and lively ways made them most popular among the younger set. The older people, in turn, soon succumbed to the wit and charm of Sophia and her husband. Before long their home became one of the most brilliant in the city.

My own brothers and sisters had also progressed in the world. Most of the older ones had married and were raising families of their own. Several of them lived in our immediate neighborhood, successful, solid tradesmen. The arrival of these sprightly foreigners brought a new joy and lightness into their rather dull lives and they became among the most regular attendants at Sophia's social gatherings.

The three youngest, Xenophon, Ysobel and Zenas, who were about the age of Sophia's three oldest, were especially charmed with the newcomers and were always to be seen in their company. It was one of the happiest moments of my life when, at a brilliant triple wedding ceremony, these six young hearts became as three.

·15·

HAPPY BIRTHDAY!

IT IS not surprising that I preferred to stay at home, surrounded by these lively young ones, rather than to accompany

Ben to his innumerable dinners and committee meetings. Now that the War was over these were very dull and unimportant affairs anyway, at which Ben seldom needed my advice. I slept through all of them and suspect that Ben usually did too.

However, I hesitated to mention my boredom lest I hurt his feelings. The approach of his eighty-first birthday promised a solution of the difficulty.

I had noticed for some time that he was becoming slightly ashamed of the old fur cap, which really *was* pretty shabby. A few days before his birthday I purchased the finest beaver hat to be found in the whole city of Philadelphia. It was a splendid affair, pale gray, turned out in the latest French fashion and just Ben's size. It cost me a pretty penny, too. In fact I had to call on my brothers Claude, Daniel and Ephraim for some financial aid, which they gladly supplied.

I told my family and Sophia's of my plans for Ben's birthday. They were overjoyed at an opportunity to show their gratitude to one who had done so much for us all and plunged into their preparations with the greatest enthusiasm.

On the eve of Ben's birthday we gathered behind the

books in his study. There was quite a crowd. All my brothers and sisters, from Bathsheba to Zenas, with their husbands, wives and children were there, as well as Sophia, her husband and *their* children. My mother and father were also present, both now quite gray, but hale and hearty as ever. All were twittering with excitement and every last one bore a present of some sort for Ben.

Prompt on the stroke of midnight, as he nodded over his writing, we swarmed forth, the children's gay voices upraised in the chorus of HAPPY BIRTHDAY TO YOU.

Ben, at first overwhelmed by surprise and pleasure, soon recovered, joining in the spirit of the occasion with the greatest gusto.

The gifts were first presented.

My mother's was a beautifully knitted earmuff. There had been time to finish only one, she explained, but the mate would be completed before cold weather set in. My father's offering was a watch charm, most skillfully gnawed from the shell of a black walnut. Sophia's was an exquisite piece of fancywork, while her husband's was a thimbleful of rare brandy, brought with him in his flight from France. This Ben gaily tossed off with a hearty toast to us all.

While the rest made their presentations, I, with twelve or thirteen of my strongest brothers, slipped quietly from the room.

Just as the last grandchild finished her little speech and curtsy, we staggered in with THE HAT.

Ben's joy knew no bounds! The gifts and honors that had been heaped upon him by the great people of foreign lands seemed as nothing, in his eyes, to the beauties of this hat!

He tried it on before the mirror and it fitted perfectly. It really didn't look bad on him, either. He insisted on wearing it all the rest of the evening, and was much amused when the younger children used its broad brim for a race track.

Crackers, cheese and ale appeared for the older folks, and barley sugar for the young ones. Then there was more singing and dancing. Sophia's eyes sparkled as she went through the graceful figures of the Minuet. I even essayed a few steps myself — with fair success. My brother Daniel's oldest girl, who was rather talented that way, recited several poems.

The climax of the entertainment came when Sophia and her husband sang, as a duet, one of Ben's poems. She had set it to music, which she had written especially for this occasion. Ben was greatly touched, and made them repeat it several times. I *did* enjoy the music.

After the happy throng had departed, I could see that Ben looked a little worried.

"Amos," he said finally: "This hat, this magnificent hat. It seems to contain no place for you. What can I do without you?"

"Ben," I said, patting his shoulder, "you can see the responsibilities I have now, all these eager young minds needing my guidance and instruction. You know that I'll always be here in the old fur cap, hanging on the bedpost, if you *really* need me. But you're eighty-one years old today, Ben. I think you're old enough to get around by yourself."

"As usual, Amos," he said, "you're right. Tomorrow I will step out and show this old town what a REAL HAT looks like!"

"All right," I said, as I curled up in the old fur cap, now all my own; "but *do* watch out for the mudholes."

[HERE THE MANUSCRIPT ENDS.]